FROM 1.0 TO 4.0

Ten Strategies for
Academic and Collegiate Success

L. TRENTON MARSH

FOREWORD BY JEFF JOHNSON

Order this book online at www.trafford.com
or email orders@trafford.com

Most Trafford titles are also available at major online book retailers.

Unless otherwise indicated, all scripture quotations are take from the **New Revised Standard Version
Bible**, copyright © 1989 National Council of the Churches of Christ in the United States of America.
Used by permission. All rights reserved.

Cover designed by Parakletos Designs.

Print information available on the last page.

ISBN: 978-1-4251-7403-3 (sc)
ISBN: 978-1-4269-9202-5 (e)

Trafford rev. 05/08/2023

 www.trafford.com

North America & international
toll-free: 844-688-6899 (USA & Canada)
fax: 812 355 4082

Believe in Yourself

Believe in yourself –
in the power you have
to control your own life,
day by day,
Believe in the strength
That you have deep inside,
and your faith will help
show you the way.
Believe in your tomorrow
and what it will bring –
let a hopeful heart
carry you through,
For things will work out
if you trust and believe
there's no limit
to what you can do.

– Emily Matthews
©AGC, Inc.

Dedication

FIRST to my *Father* that assisted in the extraction of my potential and planting the seed in me to write this guide. Next, to my Parents, Lonnie & Vivian Marsh who never gave up on me when I wanted to give up on myself. To my Pastors, Michael & Delores Freeman for exhibiting a transparent life before me which assisted me in realizing my desire to become an example and walk in integrity, character, and excellence. Next, to the men that guided me through college by living a disciplined life marked with academic rigor, who never had a clue that I was watching them – Jarrett Alexander and Adey Stembridge. And my sister, Lindsay Marsh; I am where I am because of our prayer in 1998.

A Heartfelt Thank You...

To those who contributed their time, opinion, knowledge, and acumen by providing responses to my questions about academic and collegiate success; to those that shared their inspiring academic journeys; to those that provided insightful edits, and formatting advice; as well to those that became an official sounding board during the entire process.

I do not take it lightly that you spent time to assist me; I understand that time is valuable and it is one of the few precious things that we will never get back...so I appreciate you and thank you for making time for me and this vision.

Contents

Foreword

How many of us actually believe that where we are is where we will end up? Too many of us, whether we admit it or not, are unable to see past current uncomfortable situations, bad decisions, and disappointment, to imagine self-transformation that leads to victory. Over the last 10 years I have had the great privilege to give hundreds of lectures and speeches at colleges, universities, and in local communities. There I have worked with some of the best and brightest young people the nation has to offer. Many of these best and brightest are not those with the best grades, economic privilege, or social pedigree. They are however young people, like those of you picking up this book; people with amazing potential that has yet to be realized by the most important person: YOU.

From 1.0 to 4.0: Ten Strategies for Academic and Collegiate Success is more than a set of strategies and tactics designed to improve the readers' grades, but it is the story about a journey from mediocrity to magnificence. It is a trip journal that answers questions about purpose, identity, and direction. Marsh is able, through his own experience, to provide "travel tips" that will ensure the reader has the ability to travel anywhere their dreams can imagine is possible.

I travel quite a bit and as a result find myself on airplanes more than some pilots. Because of that I love trip analogies. Try this one on and see if it fits. Many of us are on a journey from one place to another, which has been made difficult because we failed to check in early (prepare) for our flight. Because we arrive late to the airport we get placed in a middle seat, stuck between a rock and a hard place. It is that place that has too many of us motionless, unable to deal with where we are going because the ride is so uncomfortable. We often forget that even though the ride is difficult, every moment on the plane is taking us closer to our destination. No matter how long we have been going comfortably in the wrong direction we just have to **start** moving in the right direction (even when painful) to get to the right place.

If that wasn't bad enough, often when we get hungry (have desires) and the flight attendant gets to us, they are always out of the meal we want (our options seem limited). It is important to remember that what we desire has already been reserved for us if we just make the commitment to stop dreaming to crave it, and start working to claim it. I have seen students who succeeded because they never believed those that told them the world was out of what they ordered.

Even if you avoided the middle seat and brought your in-flight meal with you, some of us who think we have a direct flight (the fast track to our dreams) are really in need of a layover. A layover is when the plane lands, you let some people off the plane, get some others on the plane and refuel for the rest of the trip. Many of us have some people we *gotta* get off our plane. Some are haters, many are just negative, and a few just lack the vision to see beyond their condition. No matter the condition they are highjackers in the making. Get people *rolling* with you that want to go the same places you want to go. Finally we must find the fuel to finish the trip. For some its education, for others its training and still others need to find a place of silence that will give you the peace to renew your strength. Whatever it is find it. Remember the race goes not to the strong or the swift, but to those who can endure *til* the end. No matter the trip or the destination Marsh has prepared a handbook to help you get there

I have known Trenton Marsh for most of my life and all of his. *From 1.0 to 4.0: Ten Strategies for Academic and Collegiate Success* is not some attempt for a kid of privilege to regurgitate a message that anything is possible. This is a young man that has witnessed his own self oppression as he ignored his God given talents and abilities and nearly gave away his destiny in an attempt to possess what society told him was important (girls, popularity, and social success). Trenton is allowing us a front row seat to witness his testimony and more importantly the trials that he went through to become himself. He challenges all of us with the question: "Are you ready to be you," recognizing that YOU are synonymous with Greatness. What this book reminds all of us is no matter where we are from or what we have been through is that we have to give up that coach seat because we have a first class reservation.

Jeff Johnson, 2008
CNN Guest Correspondent
BET Host and Producer

The Mission

THE mission of this guide is simple: to produce *examples*. I want anyone that purchases this guide to apply it to their lives and use it to improve. I think the greatest position to be in is that of an *example*, because you set the pace and trend for others to replicate, and reach for similar or higher results. For generation X (those born between the years of 1965 to 1980) and generation Y (those born between the years of 1981 to 2001), one of the greatest types of people lacking in higher learning institutions, corporate America, and various arenas are males who are positive examples. Unfortunately, our society is overridden with a gluttonous and imitator instinct. It is a society that is "me" oriented. A society that tells a man that he's a "man" by having sex, and the more sex he has, the bigger the man he is. A society that tells people it's cool to fail out of school, just as long as you have the freshest sneakers and the hottest iPod™ technology before you drop out. Don't get me wrong. I know there are plenty of "good men" that serve as role models and are "other" oriented, but the question is, do generations X'ers and Y'ers see them as good men, or better, can these generations see them as true examples? Too many times, we think a "good man" is someone that represents publicly when the lights and cameras are on, but unfortunately, in the private times when integrity and character truly matter, these good men seem to turn into average men. Allow me to be an example for you as it relates to academia, collegiate, and ultimately life success. I am a man that has struggled before, both privately and publicly. This struggle was caused by a combination of lack of self control, procrastination, lazy work ethic, poor time management, and a lifestyle that was unbalanced. But all this has changed. In this guide I will demonstrate the ten strategies that I discovered that revolutionized my time management, work ethic and ultimately my grade point average. Though it took some time to achieve the success that I wanted, I had to remember the only place that you will see success before work is in the dictionary.

Introduction

MONEY. A safe neighborhood. Stay-at-home mother. Academically successful parents (Father graduated high school at 16 and went on to complete medical school; Mother graduated college and completed her Master's in Education by age 22). Intelligent siblings (oldest sister was 2nd to the Valedictorian in grade point average; other sister received full academic scholarships to attend college). Despite all of these positive influences, I still did not have academic success…but what I *did have* was success with self-gratification, comprised of women and money. For me, my success and consequently self-esteem was built upon how many girls I could "pull," or how much money I could make. That was until the spring of 1998.

You are reading a guide from a writer that went from a failing grade point average in high school to graduating at the top of his class as an undergraduate in college. I went on to pursue my Masters and became the First African American Male Commencement Speaker at The George Washington University. This means that, I was selected by the university to give an original speech at graduation to a crowd of 23,000 students, parents, family, and friends of the university. Upon graduation, and at the age of 24, the lowest salary that was offered to me was $70,000.

Now I say all this, not to be a braggadocio, but to share with you that academic and collegiate success is possible; and once you tap into academic success, life success is sure to follow. Regardless of your academic status right now (As – Fs), what I plan to share with you are my original 10 practical strategies for academic and collegiate success that I used to excel in school. These strategies focus around attitude, aptitude, and academic revolution. Connected to each strategy is an academic nugget that will bolster the strategy. You will learn how to maximize your days, impress your professors, how to become "Academically Sanctified," even how to earn an "Automatic A," amongst other things. I am well equipped to share with you how I did it, and if you so allow, how *you can do it.* This guide will be taught through a transparent lens, so I will be sharing the good, the bad, and the ugly; in fact my candor helps students evaluate where they are in life and make the necessary adjustments to obtain academic and collegiate success. I did not go from earning D's to earning a 4.0 GPA overnight; it was a 5 year process that consisted of repetition, confession, and action. But, do not be discouraged, work this process. If you make the choice to apply these 10 strategies in your life TODAY...academic and collegiate success, and ultimately life success is inevitable. Every failure and success in life begins with a conversation, and the instructions that you follow today will determine your tomorrow.

So let the conversation begin...

Part One

Locate Yourself:
Time To Navigate Your
Academic Journey

WHAT do you think is the #1 reason a person pursues higher learning?

I ask this question when I am giving presentations, and I often hear answers like, "to get good grades; to make money; to get a good job, etc." Although all these answers are okay and they certainly are byproducts. For me, however, higher learning was more than letter marks and making some money. The reality is that an institution of higher education is the place where most people develop time management skills, their work ethic, the ability to network and communicate with teams, as well as gain true confidence in becoming leaders.

The first of the 10 strategies deals with time management. I have found this to be the quintessential foundation of all success. Think about it...

A person can be a self–professed "Brainiac" in your classroom or you may know someone that has all the potential in the world but if they fail to maximize their time, or what I like to call "give life to their time"...*forget about it*! This is similar to building a house. Ask any builder or architect what is the first thing that they build. They will all say the "foundation." The foundation of a house, if done properly, will take the longest of the building process and the most discipline of the builders because they want to ensure it is strong enough to hold the structure that will be placed on top of it. So consider yourself the architect of your academic and collegiate success house, I need you to discipline yourselves in building your foundation.

There are 24 hours in a day; there are 168 hours in a week; there are 720 in a month (30 days). So what are you doing with your time? I know you have heard of the phrase "I am just killing some time." That is exactly what people are doing when they are not maximizing their time. Time is one of the few things that you will NEVER get back, so maximize, or what I like to call, *live* your time everyday. That brings us to Strategy 1.

STRATEGY 1: SUN UP – TO – SUN DOWN PRINCIPLE

This is about planning your day to day life. For this to take place, you need to write your entire schedule out the night before, with **exact hours and minutes.** I know this sounds daunting but you will be amazed to see how much you will accomplish.

I literally wrote everything down – from wake–up time, prayer, breakfast in the student dining hall, exercise at the gym, class time, library study time, professor office hour visit, lunch, phone time, washing clothes time, to playing video games as a study–break, etc. When you start preparing for life everyday with this principle this provides a solid foundation for your life. See an example below:

College Schedule

6: 15 – Wake Up	3:30 – 5:00 – Professor Office Hours
6: 20 – 6:50 – Prayer	5: 10 – 6:30 – Oceanography
7:00 – 7:30 – Workout	6:45 – 7:15 – Dinner

7: 35 – 7: 50 – Breakfast	7:30 – To room, Change Books for Library
8: 10 – 8:25 – Shower and Dress	7:45 – 9:45 – Library
8:30 – 9:45 – Spanish II	10:00 – 10:20 – Late night Snack
10: 15 – 12:00PM – Microeconomics	10:25 – 1:25AM – Library
12: 15 – 12: 45 – Lunch on campus	1:35AM – Back to room
1: 50 – 3:10 – Statistics	1:45AM – Write schedule for tomorrow

Now you try.

Think about your day tomorrow. Use the space below and write out your schedule using the Sun–up to Sun–down Principle. First start with the things you know for sure (e.g. class start and stop times) See appendix A for a spreadsheet with time slots.

Your Schedule

Academic Nugget #1: Consistency

Use the Sun–up to Sun–down principle regularly, not only am I talking about maintaining this principle on a daily basis, but also preparing your schedule for the next day at the <u>same</u> time everyday. For me it was 15 minutes before I went to sleep every night.

STRATEGY 2: NETWORK: BUILD A RELATIONSHIP WITH YOUR INSTRUCTORS

When most students think about networking they think about an event, or a moment when they have to dress up to try to impress someone with their credentials or background. But the act of net-working is not limited to a location; it is not limited to communing with someone when you want something; it is not limited to asking for a business card. Networking is a genuine way to build a rela-tionship and should be incorporated into your lifestyle. Francis Tuggle, former Dean of Argyros School of Business and Economics at Chapman University in Orange County, California says he likes "...when students ask questions, especially good questions... Outstanding questions will cause...reexamination process, some-times to completely change my viewpoints."

WHAT IS NETWORKING?

Networking does not mean brown–nosing and acting fake. People of all positions pick up on fakeness. In an institution of higher learn-ing, networking can mean:

- ▶ Staying after class to ask more questions because you are actually interested to learn.

- ▶ Making an appointment with your professor before any signs of struggle or strain in the class (if applicable) and discuss your goals and expectations of the class

- ▶ Emailing the professor about an article that ties in your reality with the material that was discussed in class

Remember that your professors are people too. They want to be asked questions about their experiences and interests as much as the next professional. When Albert Einstein was a young boy, his father did NOT ask him "Albert, what did you learn today at school?" Instead, his father asked him "Albert, did you ask any good questions today?" Here is a list of questions that you can use with some of your professors to ignite your networking experiences (this should only be used if you are interested in the course/professor…remember people pick up on phoniness):

▶ What got you interested in this area of study?

▶ What work experience do you have outside of the university that you draw from when teaching?

▶ Are there any research topics that you are currently involved in that I can assist with (only ask this if you are serious)?

Academic Nugget #2: Who you know can open doors!

As you build a relationship with your professors, inquire about letters of recommendations, internships, and summer employment opportunities. Professors have industry contacts and clout. I did not discover the value of networking until I entered graduate school, so I missed out of 4 years where I could have been networking with professors. Honestly, I was very prideful and thus ignorant to the networking concept. I thought it was **what you knew** that opened the doors, not **who you knew**…this is not entirely true. Over the years I have discovered it is **who you know** that opens the door; but it is **what you know** that keeps you there. My first job was working at The TCI Companies, an event marketing and tourism company in Washington, DC; next I was hired by Management Concepts, Inc. to do research on the training industry for the Canadian Embassy; next I interned with the Leadership Institute @ Nextel where I worked with the C–level executives…all of these positions came from Professors' contacts.

STRATEGY 3: BE ASSERTIVE: COMPLETE ASSIGNMENTS AHEAD OF SCHEDULE

Let me let you in on a little secret…many professors look at college students as immature and irresponsible. Richard Linowes, a Harvard graduate and Associate Professor of Strategic Business at the Kogod School of Business feels most college students entering into higher education are "over concerned with night life and fads." He goes on to highlight that students who "miss class without alerting their professor" and "put off assignments" are not exhibiting responsibility. But don't be offended by his comments. Hundreds of faculty members across the country believe the same thing, because this is a generalization for many students.

Patricia Hewlin, Associate Professor of Management at Georgetown University has assembled a list of behaviors that she says do not "…bode well for students, especially when they need a letter of recommendation." The behaviors are as follows:

- ▸ Not coming to class because they were "distraught" about a romantic break–up.

- ▸ Asking for a make–up to an exam for which they have no legitimate excuse for missing.

- ▸ Sleeping in class with an iPod™.

- ▸ Not pulling their weight on group assignments and expecting to receive the same credit as the others in the group who did most of the work.

- ▸ Checking email and sending text messages during class.

- ▸ Scheduling interviews on the same day of an exam.

Your responsibility as a student is to dispel and prove professors wrong.

There are two things you need to fulfill the requirements for Strategy 3:

- • A day planner with a daily calendar that is small enough that you can carry around with you at all times.

- A willingness to create and repeat confessions (more to come about this later).

THE SYLLABUS 101 OATH

At the end of strategy #3 I talked about the two things required to successfully fulfill that strategy. The latter requirement was having "a willingness to create and repeat confessions." Well, the Syllabus 101 Oath was one of the first of many confessions that I wrote, and verbally stated over and over and carried out over and over until it became a habit. I suggest you make this oath a daily part of your verbal and written regiment.

Repeat: "The first day I receive a syllabus for any class, I will go to a quiet place (hopefully your future study spot, we'll talk about this in Strategy 9) and enter every assignment due date (tests, HW, papers, etc) in my planner. If I do this I will never have any surprises. With this oath I can eradicate the famous phrase, 'I didn't know it was due.' Because I follow strategy 3 I can even start assignments before my peers."

Sylvia Black, retired Professor from University of North Carolina – Chapel Hill and North Carolina Agricultural and Techinical State University says to earn an A in her class a student "...must turn in all assignments on a timely basis, following all directions for the assignments." Dr. Black clearly would appreciate if her students utilized Strategy 3.

ACADEMIC SANCTIFICATION

So what does it take to have academic sanctification? If you were to ask your professor a question about an assignment that he hasn't even brought to the class' attention that would bring you a step closer. How do you think your professor would feel about this? I guarantee you that you have just successfully set yourself apart from your peers. The Bible calls the action of 'being set apart' as sanctification, so consider this your Academic Sanctification. When you consistently walk in this strategy, your professor no longer will see you as immature and irresponsible. In fact, when you complete assignments early, you have the advantage. I dare you to ask your professor to review your work before you submit it for the final version! I call this the "Automatic A."

Academic Nugget #3: Automatic A

As a student, I would turn in papers 3–4 weeks in advance. Why? Not because I did not have anything better to do, but because I knew my professor would review my paper for me and give me suggestions or comments about the paper. And yes you guessed it; I incorporated my professor's feedback right back into the paper. Now the caveat here is that the assignment must be high quality, this is not something that you throw together last minute and ask for a professor review. This must look like a final version.

So, if you want to earn an "Automatic A" on an assignment:

- Submit the work early (minimum 3 weeks in advance)
- Ask Professor if they would not mind reviewing your work (remember the work product must be high in quality)
- Incorporate all comments or suggestions of the Professor back into your final product

STRATEGY 4: HUMBLE YOURSELF: IF YOU DON'T KNOW SOMETHING…TELL SOMEONE!

Why struggle in class? Humility is about submission – you submitting your way of thinking to someone else and getting help. Be an introspective leader and come to grips with your strengths and areas needing improvement when it comes to your school work. Dr. Barbara Bird, Management Professor from American University in Washington, DC sums it up like this: "…I tell my students, I can't read your mind. If you are having trouble with the class, with me, with something else, you have to share that information in order to get the insights and help that others can offer." This is not easy; you will have to give up some things. In other words, delay your gratification, and focus on what is important. As a reader of this guide – your focus should be on academic and collegiate success.

DO WHAT IT TAKES TO UNDERSTAND THE MATERIAL

Skip the parties.

The parties will be there when you graduate. Now I am not saying don't have fun in school, but if you have an exam on Monday and you have not studied, but you want to go to the party on Friday... skip the party. My rule of thumb was "Play Hard...but only after Working Hard."

And yes, you will be teased. In Undergrad, I was teased by the basketball team that I sleep with my books, and not girls. They were partly correct, I slept with the girls first, then went back to the library and spent the rest of my night with my books.

Stay after class with the Professor, and set up a time to get extra help.

We talked about the importance of networking with your professors in Strategy 3, but staying after class because you are having trouble is another way to get to know (network) with your professor. If you show the tenacity to improve in an area that you once were struggling in, your professor will remember your efforts come grade reporting time.

If possible, immediately after class review your notes, and rewrite them.

Research on the brain shows that immediately applying information that was learned reinforces the information, making us more susceptible to remembering and thus have the ability to apply the knowledge. The reason, we have short and long–term memories.

According to Dr. Greg Lozier, consultant with IBM Global Business Services and expert in learner–centered training says, "If untreated, information in short–term memory begins to disappear almost immediately...short–term memory is like a buffer zone...it fills up quickly and then quickly empties."

He suggests 5 to 9 "chunks" of info can be accommodated at a time. The size of a "chunk" depends upon the prior knowledge of the learner.

That's why, professors, try to chunk things and tie things together – to reduce the load on short–term memory of a student. The less prior knowledge a person has for a subject, the faster short–term memory fills up. If the learner views the info in short–term memory as important for storage, then the info enters long–term memory. Long–term memory can be *very long* – think of the alphabet & other things you learned when you were small. Capacity of long–term memory is virtually limitless. Problem isn't storage, but retrieval.

Pay a tutor. Invest in yourself...if you don't who else will.

As students we are always quick to buy new shoes, new clothes, or other things that outwardly make us look "fly"...and that is okay, if done in the proper season. But unfortunately, we have not come to grips with investing in ourselves academically. This is beyond going to school (anyone can do that); this is beyond doing your homework on time (anyone can do that); but how many people your age do you know that have a tutor?

Unfortunately in our society we think that if a person gets a tutor they are dumb, or stupid in a particular subject matter. This is quite the contrary in my opinion.

If someone hires a tutor, to me, they are a mature, intelligent student. This student is making a conscious decision that they need help in a particular area, and they have admitted to themselves there is someone that knows the subject better than them, and consequently can teach/train them how to do better in the subject.

Go to Summer School.

Take your hardest classes in the summer; it will give you a chance to focus ONLY on one subject at a time. I know students typically think about summer vacations, and summer jobs, and that is cool too. But if one of your classes is offered in the summer, take it. I took Calculus, Statistics, Finance, and Quantitative Research Methods during summer school, and received a B+ or better in all but one of the classes. There is no question in my mind that these classes would have been a struggle for me if I took them **in addition** to 5 other courses during the regular school year.

Although I said take your hardest classes in the summer, even if the class is not hard and but it's a required course and its available in the summer...take it. Why? It keeps your mind stimulated throughout the entire year. In addition, by the time you are a senior, you would have taken your core courses and now can take elective classes (classes you are simply taking because you have an interest in them, not because you have to).

Academic Nugget #4: Barter with a tutor

If you are paying a tutor for assistance, this does not always have to be a money transaction. Bartering means trading, or exchanging services or goods for another service or good. If you do not have the cash to pay a tutor, maybe you can trade service offerings. Can you cook? Can you wash clothes? Think about the areas that you are strong in, could you trade those services?

Part Two

Ask for Directions:
Identify The Proper
Resources

THE Mentor–protégé relationships have an expansive and valuable history. The term "mentor" is actually derived from the ancient Greek character Mentor. He was a faithful friend of the Greek hero Odysseus, in Homer's epic *The Odyssey* (Wunsch, 1994). Before sailing off for the siege of Troy, Odysseus appointed Mentor to be the guardian of his household—he was to protect, advise, guide, and train his son, Telemachus, during his absence. Establishing goals for the relationship—he wanted to teach the young prince the skills needed to become a warrior, leader of men, head of household, and the future king—(Wunsch, 1994), Mentor acted faithfully for the next ten years developing and implementing the mentor–protégé relationship.

STRATEGY 5: FIND A MENTOR: WHERE THERE'S NO GUIDANCE, THERE'S NO DIRECTION

Although Homer's story reflects one of the oldest attempts by a society to facilitate mentoring, students typically in the 21st century do not see value in a mentoring relationship. In ancient Greece, it was traditionally accepted for young male citizens to be paired with older males in hopes that each boy would learn important values from his mentor. The Greeks premised these relationships on human survival—humans learn skills, culture, and values from other humans they admire (Murray, 2001). In deed, this historical concept of mentoring has a place in today's modern world.

LOOK BEYOND THE VISIBLE

Don't get caught up on the race and gender of a person! I have mentors of all races and both genders because I see something in them that I could benefit from. It may be their ability to communicate in front of large crowds, maybe their experience in a particular industry, maybe they are in a position in life that I want to be at financially, educationally, or spiritually. Often students do not want to work with someone that does not look like them. Instead of looking at the person to identify the race or gender, look for answers; successful people always leave clues.

Know there will be times when no one will look like you...so it is up to you to open the doors for those that follow. In school, I was often one of a few black students in the class, and certainly the only black male...same is true in corporate America. But I did not let that become a hindrance or an impasse to my success. Instead, it became part of the desire that has motivated me to help others succeed. I understand the value of being an example and having others look at your life to actually "see" that they can achieve as well.

Academic Nugget #5: Keep your eyes open

Think of where you want to be in life and find the people who are in those positions. How did they get there? What did they study?

There is a Biblical scripture that talks about how you should follow those who through faith and patience have inherited the promises of God[1]. This means that there will always be people who take the short–cut to what they think is success, and often times they fail. However, there are individuals that methodically plan out their lives simply by following individuals that have attained a level of life that they want. So the best way to get the same results as this person is doing exactly what they did. How do you think that would apply to you as a student?

STRATEGY 6: EVALUATE YOUR FRIENDSHIPS EVERY YEAR

When I was a freshman at American University (AU), in Washington, DC I associated with a group of 5 so–called friends… we went to clubs together, drank together, partied together, went on weekend trips, etc. When I graduated from AU four years later, I only spoke to one of those persons (and that's because he transferred to another university in DC and was about balancing his academics and having fun…not just having fun).

Not everyone will be conducive to your academic success. Friends are like a math equation: they can add to you, subtract from you, or divide you.

Write your top 4 friends down:

1.

2.

3.

4.

Mentally examine the people above…as you look at the four names above, begin to predict your future. Believe me, it is possible, just look where your friends are headed. If they are failing their tests, it won't be long for you; if they have no aspirations to study, it won't be long until that procrastination spirit gets on you; if they are dropping

---

1   Hebrews 6: 12 (NRSV)

out of school, it won't be long until you find yourself with a withdrawal slip in your hand.

This strategy seems relatively simple; many people however, fail to admit when they are in a bad friendship (relationship). As Dr. Michael A. Freeman of Spirit of Faith Christian Center reveals, "Hang with those who have your answer and get away from those who have your problem." Although a very rudimentary statement, this idea is profound – If I want to excel in school, why wouldn't I hang with people that are already successful? Why wouldn't I try to mimic their actions (study habits, networking, buying the 1.0 to 4.0 guide, etc.), at least until I was in a position to create my own path? Why would I stay around friends that shared my same bad habits (no work ethic, laziness, procrastinator, etc.), and often times worse off than I?

You can implement this same strategy into your future career. If you want to be a doctor when you graduate from your higher institution, why not start preparing now? Why not intern at a local doctor's office, or offer to volunteer your spare time at a hospital? If you think that you may be interested in politics, why not go to your local congress person's office and inquire about obtaining an internship? This type of tenacity is for any career, any educational path, etc. So what are you doing with your interests?

There is a Proverb that states "Make no friends with those given to anger[2]." Here anger connotes an uncontrollable temper, but anger is also representative of anything that is not representative of YOU. So, think about my earlier statement about being able to predict your own future based upon your friends. Meditate on that statement for a moment. In fact, if you show me your friends I can predict your future. I just said if you physically show me your friends, I can dictate to you how your future will be simply based upon the company you keep. Bad friendships will block your ability to grow and maximize your successes in every area of your life – academically, financially, socially, professionally, and most importantly, spiritually. When something is not growing there are only two alternatives: stagnation and death. Why would anyone allow their pursuit of academic and collegiate success be determined and detained by an unhealthy friendship?

---

2   Proverbs 22:24 (NRSV)

Academic Nugget #6: Leverage friends

The term leverage is often used in financial settings, such as banks or mortgage lending institutions, but in the realm of academic success, we will use the *American Heritage Dictionary's* definition, which is "positional advantage...to improve or enhance." You may have friends that took the same course that you are taking, maybe not with the same instructor, but the same content and materials nonetheless. So leverage your friends! Ask for their class notes, old homework assignments, teacher handouts, and articles, these documents will give you a competitive advantage. See below for some examples how you could leverage a friend's old documentation.

Articles

- Read it!

- Examine how have things changed? Focus on the respective industry, government, laws, etc. that the old article focuses on. How can you relate the article with the present year?

Homework, Class notes

- Use the questions as additional study material and practice problems.

- Incorporate definitions, questions, etc. that are new to you in your study guide for your examinations and quizzes.

Teacher Handouts

- Read it!

- After reading the article, bring the handout to the teacher's attention and engage in a dialogue (Remember Strategy #2)

There are other documents that you could leverage but the question is whether your professor/teacher approves them as "review" documentation; these could include old examinations, old quizzes, old papers, etc. Before using **any** of these items ask your professor for their opinion and approval.

Finally, it is important to highlight and remember leveraging does not equate to cheating. I am convinced those that resort to cheating, 1.) Lack integrity 2.) Are lazy, causing them not to prepare; and this translates into 3.)Not having self–confidence in their personal ability to succeed.

STRATEGY 7: USE FREE HELP: GO TO THE LIBRARY, LIBRARIANS GET PAID TO HELP YOU

Do not imitate my first 3 months in college; I never stepped foot in the library. However by the time I graduated, I spent most of my time there. Often times students do not take advantage of the free resources that are at their disposal. Jennifer Nutefall, Director of Instruction, at the Gelman Library at The George Washington University, and former Librarian at SUNY Brockport in New York has been instructing students and faculties on research for 9 years. She believes the #1 reason why incoming freshmen do not use the free resource [librarians]: "...they feel they should be able to do the research themselves and it is hard to admit they need assistance." She goes on to say that, "Students realize a lot of information is available online and...use the article databases to find that information..." Students typically fail to realize that their university library has a much larger budget and subscribes to many more resources than were available to them in high school.

Before entering an institution of higher learning, Ms. Nutefall recommends all students be familiar with the following research engines, as they provide a solid foundation on academic research:

Academic Search Premier
Proquest Research Library
InfoTrac

During college, students should become aware of the main article databases in their respective fields, as well as the major professional association. Otherwise this puts them at a disadvantage when searching for information. Most librarians appreciate it when students come prepared before approaching them for assistance. Included in

Appendix B is the *Librarian Assistance Diagnostic,* which will assist you in articulating your assignment to the librarian.

Academic Nugget #7: Wisdom vs. Foolishness: Keep Wise Counsel

When I purchased my first house I needed advice, so I contacted a real estate agent. Similarly, when I created an investment portfolio, I reached out to another professional, a financial planner to assist me. When I started my first business and had questions concerning taxes on businesses, I phoned my accountant. When there are legal questions, I call upon my lawyer. All these professionals are a group that I call my "wise counsel," I reach out to them when I need help and don't know something, or when I want to bounce ideas of them. In all these situations it would have been foolish of me not to seek the counsel. Just like it's foolish for you to think that you do not need the library or the librarian's assistance to do well in school. It's foolish, and prideful, to think you have all the answers.

Who is in your wise counsel? If you have never thought about it, you should start now, because the list grows and matures as you grow and mature. Just like I have a wise counsel concerning professional/financial inquiries, you should have a wise counsel at your university. Brainstorm below, who's in your counsel? I will give you a head start with putting at least two people in the list for you:

1. Academic Advisor/Guidance Counselor

2. Librarian (*aka* Reference Accountant)

3.

4.

5.

6.

Part Three

Get Comfortable: Avoid Unnecessary Layovers

D ISCOVER the comfort and peace of studying in a consistent location. There is something about going to the same location when preparing for an examination, solving a difficult equation, or writing a paper. Proper preparation prevents poor performance, and I believe your study place is connected to your performance.

STRATEGY 8: FIND A STUDY PLACE... AND KEEP IT!

As an undergraduate, my place was the basement of the library, in the back by discontinued journals. As a graduate student it was at a table in the "Quiet Room," this is a location in a university library where no groups can meet, no cell phones can be used, and sometimes laptops are not permitted.

University Professors also value a consistent location. I asked Dr. Michael Marquardt, writer, researcher, and Professor at The George Washington University about his "work space" and its importance. He reveals, "I do all of my research and writing at my home office. At the GWU office, there are too many interruptions, not enough private time and space." Dr. Marquardt is the author of the award-winning text "Action Learning." Even Professors value the importance of a work space. Regardless of your choosing, choose one location.

Academic Nugget #8: Be honest with yourself

Unless you live by yourself with no windows and no electronics, food, etc. do not study in your dorm room or house. There are too may distractions that you may subconsciously forget – your roommate, your family members, your TV, your iPod™, your cozy bed, etc.

STRATEGY 9: GET UP! TAKE CONSCIOUS STUDY BREAKS

Do not burn out. Make sure to write study breaks in your daily schedule (Sun–up to Sun–down Principle #1), perhaps a quick video game, watching your favorite television show, or taking a quick nap. But remember it's just a break…don't let 30 minutes turn into 3 hours.

Academic Nugget #9: Do not underestimate sleep

Donnell Baldwin, a personal trainer and formerly with *Washington Sports Club, Inc.* before starting his own fitness company, says sleep is important. "During our resting/sleeping period our bodies rejuvenate, repairs and restores itself and allows our muscles to grow (especially if you're working out regularly)." He includes that resting "significantly aids in mental acuity" so that we are able to remain sharp and focused during the course of the day. Mr. Baldwin's advice,

"Try going to bed by no later than 10:30pm for a week. I guarantee that you'll feel refreshed!"

STRATEGY 10: BALANCE IS ESSENTIAL; BOOKS AND EXTRACURRICULAR ACTIVITIES

Before you graduate from your institution of higher learning, make sure you are involved in activities that expand outside of your class-work. This is what job recruiters look for. As a student you should be involved in leadership development through student–led organizations, involved in spiritual growth, as well as social growth. Candi Waller, University Recruiter for IBM Corporation agrees. She says that "Recruiters love to see well rounded students. It is a pleasure to speak with students that are leaders in the classroom, as well as, in their communities and extracurricular activities." Nasya Khanna, Recruiter for Keepers, Inc., a technology contracting firm says she finds that "Career minded... students who have a lot of potential are usually more flexible..."

As a volunteer recruiter for university hires in corporate America I too, am drawn to the "flexible" student, one who had a 3.0 GPA **along with** a host of activities on their resume (President, member of organization, volunteer tutor, etc.) over a 4.0 ONLY GPA student that was not involved with anything. For me, the student with the 3.0 has shown time management, work ethic, leadership, and the ability to network. The person with a 4.0 only exhibited the ability to be a good student in a classroom environment.

Academic Nugget #10: Be productive, not just active

How many people do you know that are always on the run, or always involved with an activity? It seems they are always busy with something. I would argue that the majority of these folks are just being active, but not productive. There is a significant difference, and the key ingredient is passion. When you tap into your passion, some refer to it as purpose in life, this is an inward feeling that you have that what you are doing is so enjoyable, at times it does not feel like you are working. Donald Grant, top Regional Sales Manager at Xerox Corporation, presents the inward feeling like this, "Your passion is your purpose in life; and when you find it you should ask yourself if money was not an issue could I do this for the rest of my life? If the answer is yes, then welcome to your passion."

When you tap into passion you will not join any and every organization. You will not give your time to activities that do not serve a purpose in your life. Why? , Because you will give life to your time and focus on activities that are connected with your passion and fulfilling of your purpose.

Part Four

Arriving at Your Destination: Experience Others' Academic Journeys

REMEMBER success is a process. I did not go from failing classes to being at the top of my class and giving speeches in front of large audiences overnight...you will have to delay your gratification and patiently apply these strategies. Dr. Adey Stembridge, former Director of the McNair Scholars program in Washington, DC says "Students expect glory without pain and hard work..." but, he adds "To be fair; there are many students who have it right." From Law, to Engineering, to Public Health, to English, below is a sampling of individuals that applied the 1.0 to 4.0 strategies and have received success in both their academics and their personal lives.

R. Sinha – Bachelors of Science in Mechanical Engineering, George Washington University

Ms. Sinha approached me concerning how to change her grade point average around, as she was on the brink of academic probation in the school of engineering. At the time I was a graduate student taking education and business coursework and was at the core of applying every strategy in this guide.

"Having a Mechanical Engineering major and a Japanese Language minor, I faced several academic roadblocks and disappointments as a college student. The first few years in my program, I obtained near a 1.0 GPA a few times and was placed on academic probation several times. I desperately wanted to rescue my GPA and I tried every resource available. At that time, I personally knew L. Trenton Marsh, as he was a Graduate student at my University. I was aware that he was a 4.0 student and one day I took time to inquire with him on what steps he was taking to maintain his academic success. He encouraged me and shared with me the very principles that are found in this book because during that time, these were the steps he was taking personally. I slowly began to see an improvement in my academic performance and am very proud to say I achieved a 4.0 GPA my last year of Undergraduate studies. I am currently in Law School and looking forward to implementing the same strategies to ensure my success."

K. Butler – 2 Year Law Student, University of Michigan

When I was approached by Ms. Butler about how to be successful in law school I told her about Strategy # 10. She already expressed to me her scholastic aptitude, so I wanted to ensure there were other activities that balanced her academic acumen especially at a "majority" institution.

"This summer [2007] I asked you for advice on how to be successful in graduate school and you gave me three pointers that seem simple on their face, but have proven to help keep me grounded in this extreme environment:

1.   Attend church regularly

2.   Get involved with a Black Graduate School organization on campus

3.   Continue in prayer

This has been very helpful to me in my pursuit of success in law school. I know that in the future I will be able to attribute a good portion of my academic success to your advice. Thanks again."

Y. Orji – Masters of Arts in Public Health, George Washington University

I have known Ms. Orji for several years and I've always known her to be extremely active in many activities, but with that said, I've also known her to get distracted when it came to being a student...because of the countless activities.

"As with most people, Time Management had been a challenge of mine. I hadn't mastered the concept in Undergrad when my real main objective was to be a student first, and then engage in extra curricular activities second. So by the Time I started my Master's Degree, while simultaneously working full time—I HAD TO GET IT TOGETHER!

I was what you would call a "Chronic Procrastinator (CP)." and it wasn't that I didn't care about my work, or didn't want to do it; it was just that I didn't have a PLAN or strategy of approach on the BEST way to do the work. Those who suffer from CP often believe that they have more time than they think to do the work or minimize the magnitude of the assignment.

At the root of my chronic procrastinating was organization, or a lack thereof. In undergrad, I hardly ever used a planner. Instead, I kept a running Tally of tasks and agenda items in my head, which often got pushed to the side the minute something more appealing presented itself. Without Discipline and organization, procrastination was inevitable.

So in Grad School, as the requests for extensions grew, I knew I had to face my problem head on (I knew it was BAD when as punishment for a late paper, I had to write an additional paper on procrastination...which also was handed in slightly late...)

Insert L. Trenton Marsh. I knew I had a problem (Not like a crack problem... but a problem nonetheless). My life had not balance, no control. I felt like I spent SOO much time putting in work... but at the end of the day... I couldn't account for any progress that was made! I was in a sense, "Doing Much of nothing!"

Trenton's Treatment:

1). GET A PLANNER!

2). Write EVERYTHING down!

3). Write due dates weeks in advance so that you can put in the work early and have enough time to get appropriate feed back from the professor.

4) Decide what is IMPORTANT! Cut back on extracurricular activities and recognize the position you are currently in--and that was to be a student and an employee firstly, everything else...is EXTRA

Trenton's Treatment was EXACTLY what I needed! While I have not yet been able to give a professor a paper three weeks in advance, my requests for extensions has DRASTICALLY reduced! Now my planner is my best friend! It keeps me organized, and I'm able to find some

sense of order in my daily work! Baby steps... in the
RIGHT DIRECTION!"

S. Fitzpatrick, Bachelors of Arts in English, George Washington University

I met Mr. Fitzpatrick when he was a sophomore at GWU and I was
impressed immediately with what seemed to be a strong worth ethic.
After connecting with him on various levels, I knew he would be active
on campus, bringing empowerment to those that needed it most.

"After graduating high school in the top 2% of my class,
I matriculated to The George Washington University,
where I am currently a senior honors student. As part of
my admission, I was awarded the Presidential Academic
Scholarship, and I am now also a member of several
scholastic honor societies including The National Society
of Collegiate Scholars and Golden Key International
Honour Society. Most importantly, I will be graduating
a full semester early, and will be receiving two degrees
from GW and Georgetown University. How did all of
this come to pass you ask? Well, first and foremost, all
the praise, honor, and glory belong to GOD because
HE has blessed me tremendously. HE also placed me on
a path upon which I encountered Mr. Trenton Marsh.
Trenton introduced me to a principle that revolutionized
the way I approached one area of my life that has
always been less than excellent: time management. Mr.
Marsh's [strategy] is called the *Sun–Up, Sun–Down*
principle, and I now utilize it to maximize nearly every
aspect of my undergraduate life. By way of my adopting
Trenton's principle, everything from organizing my
weekly schedule to structuring my "unstructured" free–
time has become far less difficult, and I no longer feel
overwhelmed by the fast–paced lifestyle that I lead as
an undergraduate student living, working, and interning
in the Nation's Capital. I first heard Trenton elucidate
his principle when I attended his workshop, which is

entitled "From a 1.0 to a 4.0." I have since heard him speak on several occasions, most recently at the Man 2 Man Conference for young Black men which took place in Anacostia High School in Southeast DC, and can honestly attest to the fact that Mr. Marsh's strategies for academic and personal success have completely altered my perspective with regard to what can be accomplished in the 24 hours that we are given to work with each day."

A. Okanlawon, Bachelors of Arts in Psychology, George Washington University

Ms. Okanlawon was an audience member at a College–Unplugged event where the panelists talked about the hush items of college. My topic was on the importance of academic success as soon as you get to college.

"I was definitely one of the many who write papers/do assignments a day or two before they are due. Well, I set myself to do my BEST this semester in school and as commonly stated, "If you want new results, you have to try new things". At a College Un–plugged panel event I heard Trenton's [1].0–4.0 story and his advice on how to make it happen for myself. One of the [strategies] he proposed was turning in papers at least [three] weeks or so in advance so the professor could then look over it, correct it, and hand it back to you to correct. With this done, you have the opportunity to enhance your grade. So, I tried it...the professor said my paper was great...I did not have to re–do it...and I got an A! Glory be to God! I am on my way to that 4.0."

Part Five

1.0 to 4.0 Academic Transformation Credo

SIMILAR to a Greek or fraternal organization, a trade or civic association, or a social club, most people who share like–minded belief systems or ideals recite confessions, oaths, mission statements, or credos. One organization in particular that I like its credo is for the *American Entrepreneurs Association, 1987.*

> "I do not choose to be a common person. It is my right to be uncommon––if I can. I seek opportunity B not security. I do not wish to be a kept citizen, humbled and dulled by having the state look after me.
>
> I want to take the calculated risk, to dream and to build, to fail and to succeed.
>
> I refuse to barter incentive for a dole; I prefer the challenges of life to the guaranteed existence; the thrill of fulfillment to the stale calm of Utopia.

I will not trade my freedom for beneficence nor my dignity for a handout. I will never cower before any master nor bend to any threat.

It is my heritage to stand erect, proud and unafraid; to think and act for myself, to enjoy the benefit of my creations and to face the world boldly and say: "This, with God's help, I have done."

All this is what it means to be an Entrepreneur."

If aspiring and current entrepreneurs have a credo, why not aspiring and current scholars; turn to the next page for the *1.0 to 4.0 Credo* that I have created just for you. Elements of the credo come from Appendix C, *Academic Transformation Statements* that I focused on as a student.

1.0 TO 4.0 ACADEMIC TRANSFORMATION CREDO

I, _____ am created in the image and likeness of God. I am designed to dominate and I am engineered for excellence. No one can define who I am but me and the one who created me. My past academic history, motivation, time management skills, etc. does not dictate my future. In fact, my academic and life success will be fulfilled because I am a doer; not a hearer and reader only. I will positively influence the lives of those who are around me, to cause their lives to be impacted forever. Everything that I touch prospers. Everything that I speak comes to pass. My life will follow my thoughts and words, so I will be careful with both. I know success is a process; therefore I will not fail, but I will continue to grow in my academic and collegiate success.

I will apply the following 10 strategies as well as the nuggets, academic journeys and study tips that I learned in this guide to be successful:

Strategy 1: Sun up – to – Sun down Principle

Strategy 2: Network: Build a relationship with your Instructors

Strategy 3: Be assertive: Complete assignments ahead of schedule.

Strategy 4: Humble yourself: If you don't know something…Tell someone!

Strategy 5: Find a Mentor: Where there's no guidance, there's no direction

Strategy 6: Evaluate your friendships EVERY year

Strategy 7: Use free help: Go to the library, librarians get paid to help you

Strategy 8: Find a study place…and keep it!

Strategy 9: Get Up! Take conscious study breaks

Strategy 10: Balance is essential; Books and Extracurricular Activities.

Guardian/Teacher/Mentor	Your Name	Date

Part Six

Study Tips –
Beyond Memorization

INDIVIDUAL study methods can vary greatly depending upon a student's major However, there are some basic foundational principles that can be utilized regardless of your discipline.

- *Start early.* Procrastination is an enemy of success.

- *Consistency.* This deals with studying. The way a person has handled the class all year should be proper preparation come the time for an exam, test, or quiz.

- *Review.* Go back over old assignments, homework, quizzes, and exams and look over the questions you got incorrect and if you do not know the reason it was marked wrong ask your professor to review the answers with you.

- *Groups.* If a class is a challenge, pair up with someone who knows the content much better. Remember strategy #9. Identify people, places and grades you

> want to have…hang with or get help from these
> people.

Now that we have covered the basic principles, we will get into some discipline specific questions that I have encountered over a period of time while giving speeches and presentations to various student and alumni audiences. The next section covers a multitude of disciplines, and highlights individuals who discovered study habits that allowed them to achieve academic success. See the questions that were asked and read the responses. As with all advice, extract what works for you!

PHYSICS

Name: M. Ojaruega
Major/Discipline of Study: Experimental Nuclear Physics
Institutions and their Location (Present, if applicable and Past):
> University of the District of Columbia, Washington, DC
> The University of Michigan–Ann Arbor, MI

Degree Name and Type (Present, if applicable and Past):
> BS–Physics
> MS. Physics
> Ph.D. (estimated December 2008)

Current Occupation: Doctoral Student in applied nuclear physics
Desired Occupation upon graduation:
> College professor and assist law/policy makers understand the importance of science

I. **As a student what specific steps do you take to prepare for an exam? What is the order (please be as detailed as possible)?**

> Well, for examinations, I usually start my preparation
> about 10 days in advance…I don't like to be rushed hence
> I start early. Usually, I would follow my notes before
> looking at the text book…I have a rule that, no studying

a day and a half before exams. I really spend a lot of time after class going over materials…just so I don't have to cram things. When studying physics, memorization is not the way to in this case…understand fundamentals and derivations is really the way. That is why I give my self time to understand concepts early in the class and usually the exams would test both conceptual materials and mathematics…I spend about three hours going over each class I attend. I also randomly read sections of already covered chapters in class just for clarity.

2. **How did you discover your study preparation, did you read a book? Receive advice? Please explain your response.**

I discovered I had to study hard when I was in middle school. In college however, my advisor told me during my sophomore year that I had to spend two hours for every hour of lecture. This habit followed me all the way to graduate school. I realized I was good at retaining information through writing and also good at matching numbers. Because of this, when I read books, even novels, I write the information down. I retain information more thoroughly when I am writing it down. That seems to be how my brain functions. I really never read a book about how to study or prepare. I just know that from an early age from both my siblings and family that, to make it in school one had to study. That's what I did. And to be honest, I had a friend when I was growing up who always made good grades. He attended a different school than I did. One day I asked him after about a couple of years of wondering, I asked him, " How come you are so smart, you get all "A"s and all the awards?" He looked at me and said "All I do is just study until I get it and quit." Those words changed my view of learning. Since then, I focused on understanding. And truth be told, I never deviated from that simple advice. I still follow it today. And that friend now calls me "The smartest Nuke scientist."

3. **Do you think there is some validity in the statement that college students are immature and irresponsible? Please explain your response.**

There is definitely some truth to that statement, but not entirely. A lot of the undergraduates are products of their environment. You are what you take inside of you. Better yet, you are what you read! Most of the students are coming to college with one mindset. I am free from my parents' control; hence they really forget to some extent that they are responsible for a lot of their actions. This is so because their parents have always been there for them prior to college. On the other hand, some students come in with lots of experience. They've had to grow up faster than the average or typical "American high school student" Now I am referring to some international students that have had lots of responsibilities prior to coming to college. Some of these students have been business partners with their parents, farmers and they are really focused. These students usually have a good sense of what is expected of them as students, and moreover that, they feel like they represent their entire extended family, regardless of where they are.

4. **In your estimation how could a prospective or current student earn/achieve an "A" grade in a class in your discipline?**

So, to earn an A in Physics, a student must work on the skill to visualize a problem and be able to draw the geometry. Ask lots of questions. Usually that clears up lots of misunderstanding in physics. Students should utilize professor's office hours to their advantage. To get an A, you must really understand fundamental concepts. All branches of physics are based on the key fundamentals. It's like a house...for it to be solid; you must have a strong foundation. The foundation in physics are the basic fundamentals like conservation of energy and momentum.

LAW

Full Name: R. Singh
Major/Discipline of Study: Psychology, minor in Africana Studies
Institutions and their Location (Present, if applicable and Past):
    The George Washington University, Washington, DC
    Syracuse University College of Law, Syracuse, NY
    Saint Louis University School of Law, St. Louis, MO

Degree Name and Type (Present, if applicable and Past):
    BA in Psychology
    Juris Doctorate
    Master's in Letter of Law, Health Law

Current Occupation: Attorney

1. **As a student what specific steps do/did you take to prepare for an exam? What is the order (please be as detailed as possible)?**

    I reviewed my notes and prepared a robust study guide.

2. **How did you discover your study preparation, did you read a book? Receive advice? Please explain your response.**

    No one taught me how to study. I did not read any books on study preparation. I tried my study method the first time and it worked.

3. **Do you think there is some validity in the statement that college students are immature and irresponsible? Please explain your response. If you believe this statement has validity how would you recommend students overcome?**

    There is some validity to that statement. Some students come to college and think just because their parents are not hovering over them, they can act wild: not go to class, not study, etc. There is nothing like having fun in college. That's part of the experience. If a student realizes that what he/she does in college will determine their future, I think they will act more mature and responsible.

4. **In your estimation how could a prospective or current student earn/achieve an "A" grade in a class in your discipline?**

    Read the assigned reading material, take notes, review your notes weekly, make outlines/study guides, and ask the professor questions if you do not understand something.

MATH AND ACCOUNTING

Full Name: A. Sledge
Major/Discipline of Study: Mathematics/Accounting
Institutions and their Location (Present, if applicable and Past):
    University of Pittsburgh, Pittsburgh, PA
    Keller Graduate School of Management, Cleveland, OH

Degree Name and Type (Present, if applicable and Past):
    Bachelor of Science, Mathematics
    Master of Accounting and Financial Management (Spring 08)

Current Occupation: Middle School Math Teacher and Real Estate
Investor

Desired Occupation upon graduation (if applicable):
Certified Public Accountant

1. **As a student what specific steps do/did you take to prepare for an exam? What is the order (please be as detailed as possible)?**

   To prepare for an exam, specifically for an undergraduate mathematics exam, I would go to the math library at my university or to the math help desk. I utilized all my notes and sample problems from class and rework quiz problems, proofs and homework until I felt comfortable with the material. Also studied with like minded students, people that not only looked like me, but also wanted to do exceptionally well in the class.

2. **How did you discover your study preparation, did you read a book? Receive advice? Please explain your response.**

   In discovering my study preparation, I found that earning good grades was all the motivation I needed to excel. It was such a great feeling knowing that all the time and preparation put into studying would ultimately benefit me in the long–run. Moreover, I received valuable advice from my primary and secondary schoolteachers early on about the importance of maintaining good study habits and work ethics.

3. **Do you think there is some validity in the statement that college students are immature and irresponsible? Please explain your response. If you believe this statement has validity how would you recommend students overcome?**

There is some validity in the statement that some college students are immature and irresponsible. College students are independent for the first time without parental supervision, thus they have a feeling of being in control due to gaining a sense of freedom. The opportunity to be independent can be a little overwhelming for some immature students which in turn cause them to behave and act irresponsibly. Consequently, students may enter into credit card debt and excessive partying. Early on, I would recommend that such students seek a mentor or a sophisticated student for wisdom and support.

4. **In your estimation how could a prospective or current student earn/achieve an "A" grade in a class in your discipline?**

One could certainly earn an "A" in the study of mathematics by reviewing concepts daily, meeting with the professor during office hours, and not being afraid of a challenge. Furthermore, by asking questions and taking advantage of all resources and opportunities needed to succeed, students may do an exceptional job in math or any math–based discipline such as accounting.

ENGINEERING

Full Name: K. Broadnax
Major/Discipline of Study: Engineering
Institutions and their Location (Present, if applicable and Past):
North Carolina Agricultural and Technical State University,
Greensboro, NC

Degree Name and Type (Present, if applicable and Past):
Bachelors of Science, Engineering (concentration in Physics)

Current Occupation: Physicist working for NavAIR

I.   **As a student what specific steps do you take to prepare for an exam? What is the order (please be as detailed as possible)?**

NEVER studied alone. Classes were very small, so we always stuck together as a group to study. What one person didn't know, someone else did. Learned Teamwork. Reviewed ALL homework problems because tests encompassed problems similar to Homework. Completed homework together as a group. Was prepared to be up all night before the test, took naps earlier in the day to prepare for all–nighter. "Grind" all night.

2.   **How did you discover your study preparation, did you read a book? Receive advice? Please explain your response.**

Discovered this process freshmen year in college when faced with a very challenging Physics course, and failed the first test. Everyone in class failed test individually. That is when everyone realized that group studying would help each classmate. Everyone was in same classes together and we all matriculated into more advanced classes together also.

3. **Do you think there is some validity in the statement that college students are immature and irresponsible? Please explain your response.**

    Disagree with the statement that college students are immature and irresponsible; depends on individual student's personality, environmental upbringing, choice of friends. That statement is too general and cannot be applicable to ALL college students. There are too many factors that encompass the makeup of one's maturity level.

4. **In your estimation how could a prospective or current student earn/achieve an "A" grade in a class in your discipline?**

    By putting forth EXTRA effort. Going to Office Hours. Get to class early. Taking notes. Really doing the reading in the book not just read notes after class. Complete homework the SAME day it is assigned.

References

American Entrepreneurs Association Official Credo, 1987

Murray, M. (2001). *Beyond the myths and magic of mentoring.* Jossey–Bass San Francisco, CA: Business.

The American Heritage® Dictionary of the English Language, 4th ed. Boston: Houghton Mifflin, 2000.

Wunsch, M.A. (1994). *Mentoring revised: Making an impact on individuals and institutions.* San Francisco, CA: Jossey–Bass.

http://www.gwu.edu/gelman/ref/appoint.html
(George Washington University, Gelman Library [Available online])

About the Author

ORIGINALLY from Shaker Heights, Ohio Trenton Marsh transitioned to Washington, DC in 1998 as a student at American University (AU) where he received several awards based upon his leadership and academic accomplishments. A few include the William Randolph Hearst Scholarship and the Frank J. Luchs Memorial Scholarship. Marsh was also inducted into the Golden Key International Honor Society for being in the top 15% of his graduating class; a major feat considering in high school he once had a "D" grade point average. He graduated from AU with an Honors BSBA degree double–majoring in Marketing and Enterprise Management in May 2002.

Upon graduation Marsh went on to pursue his Master's degree in Education and Human Resource Development from the George Washington University (GW), also in Washington, DC. He continued his academic success, earning an impressive 3.97 GPA and several academic scholarships, including the Anna Spicker Hampel Award and the Dr. Delores A. Freeman Scholarship. Marsh assumed many leadership roles while attending GW. His most cherished was his Presidency of the re–organized Black Graduate Student Association (BGSA), in which he turned a defunct organization of 5 members into a strong voice on campus with over 140 members within one year. That year BGSA was recognized with a nomination for the *GW Excellence Award for Student Organization of the Year (2003–2004)*. Individually Marsh was recognized with a nomination for the *Dr. Martin Luther King, Jr. Medal (2003–2004 and 2004–2005)*, an award recognizing GW's most respected student leaders. In May of 2004, Marsh made history at GW when he became the First African American Male Commencement Speaker, speaking to a crowd of

23,000 people on the Ellipse (the land between the White House and the Washington Monument).

Upon graduation, Marsh created the GW Black Alumni Association to foster a sense of community among black alumni by creating an immovable network of successful black graduates. By supporting their academic, professional, social and spiritual growth through networking events, speaker series and professional development; in one year membership grew close to 200 alumni. Marsh was also invited to speak at the 100th Anniversary Celebration for the Graduate School of Education and Human Development (GSEHD) at The George Washington University. Recently GSEHD invited him to speak to the National Advisory Council at the Carnegie Institute in Washington, DC.

Marsh's lifestyle and community involvement has garnered the attention of many notable entities including: The *MTV network*, as the producers of MTV's True Life Series interviewed Marsh for their series on lifestyle of celibacy; *Essence Magazine*, as he was nominated for the "Mr. Do Right 2007," an honor given to single men who inspire and work hard at making an impact in their communities; and also the *CNN Network*, as he was featured in CNN. com's "Young People Who Rock," which recognizes people between the ages of 21–30 for their community involvement, leadership, and desire to change the world.

Understanding the importance of a strong education, Marsh co-founded *CommitMEN* in 2005, an organization dedicated to closing the achievement gap of African American males in college. He currently serves as the Director of Strategic Alliances for *CommitMEN*, helping to raise scholarships (from personal finances and corporate match programs) to send black males to college and mentor them during their collegiate experience. Despite a busy work schedule, Marsh is active in both the community and his church. He serves as a leader and role model for many other young adult singles and youth. He continues to empower young men and women by speaking to them about mapping a road to success and using himself as an example of what spiritual guidance, determination, and perseverance can do.

Appendix

APPENDIX A: SUN–UP TO SUN–DOWN MATRIX

HOW DO YOU SPEND YOUR 168 HOURS A WEEK?

Time	Sunday	Monday	Tuesday	Wednesday	Thursday	Friday	Saturday
6:00 to 7:00							
7:00 to 8:00							
8:00 to 9:00							
9:00 to 10:00							
10:00 to 11:00							
11:00 to 12:00							
12:00 to 1:00							
1:00 to 2:00							
2:00 to 3:00							
3:00 to 4:00							
4:00 to 5:00							
5:00 to 6:00							
6:00 to 7:00							
7:00 to 8:00							
8:00 to 9:00							
9:00 to 10:00							
10:00 to 11:00							
12:00 to 1:00							
1:00 to 2:00							

APPENDIX B: LIBRARIAN ASSISTANCE DIAGNOSTIC

Courtesy of George Washington University,
http://www.gwu.edu/gelman/ref/appoint.html

APPENDIX C: ACADEMIC TRANSFORMATION STATEMENTS

The statements below are real. In college, I said these every morning when I woke up and every night before I went to bed. I had them posted on my bathroom mirror, on my wall next to my bed, on light switches, and even on my refrigerator. Everywhere I turned there was a positive affirmation of my goals to have academic and life success. You may use the statements; you may use none of them, but allow them to be a template or measurement for you as you generate your successes.

- I will earn a 4.0 GPA this semester and beyond
- I am just like Daniel[3], I, too, am 10x better than all the students in my classes
- Just like David[4], I have success in all my undertakings
- I believe that I have work/life balance so I can lead successful organizations and have success in the classroom

---

3   Daniel 1
4   1 Samuel 18

Printed in the United States
by Baker & Taylor Publisher Services